This edition published by Parragon in 2013
Parragon
Chartist House
15–17 Trim Street
Bath BA1 1HA, UK
www.parragon.com

Copyright © Parragon Books Ltd 2012

ISBN 978-1-4723-1078-1

Printed in China

The Little Mermaid

Retold by Ronne Randall

Illustrated by Dubravka Kolanovic

PaRragon

Bath • New York • Cologne • Melbourne • Delhi
Hong Kong • Shenzhen • Singapore • Amsterdam

Once upon a time, deep beneath the sea, there lived a lovely little mermaid. She had long, chestnut hair, deep-sea-blue eyes, and a beautiful fishtail of silvery green. She also had a voice as clear and bright as crystal, the most beautiful voice in the ocean.

The Little Mermaid lived with her father, the Sea King, and her five older sisters. She spent her days playing near their castle and singing to the other sea creatures.

On a mermaid's fifteenth birthday, she is allowed to go to the surface of the sea to watch the human world.

When it was the Little Mermaid's turn, she swam up eagerly.

A ship was sailing nearby. As the Little Mermaid listened to the music and laughter, she saw a handsome young prince. The Little Mermaid looked at him and felt her heart melt with love.

The Little Mermaid followed the ship from a distance, so that she could watch the young prince.

Suddenly, lightning FLASHED across the sky and thunder CRACKED.

A fierce storm blew up, and the ship tossed and turned in the waves.

The Little Mermaid watched as it sank, hoping that the prince was safe.

When the storm was over, the Little Mermaid saw
her prince at last. He was lying in the water
with his eyes closed, too tired to swim.

"I must save him," the Little Mermaid thought.

She swam to him and took him to the safety of the shore. There she sang to him in her lovely, sweet voice until he opened his eyes.

He caught only a glimpse of her before she darted away to hide in the water.

Before long, a pretty girl came down to the beach. She found the prince and helped him up.

The Little Mermaid watched them walk away together. Then, with an aching heart, she swam back to her home.

With tears in her eyes, the Little Mermaid told her sisters that she had fallen in love with the prince. They knew who he was, and took her to see his home—a castle the color of sand, with steps winding down to the sea.

After that, the Little Mermaid swam to the surface every day to watch the prince. "I would do anything to be human so that he might fall in love with me," she told her sisters.

Finally, her sisters said, "Go and visit the Sea Witch. Perhaps she can help you."

The Sea Witch lived in a dark, underwater forest, amid slimy plants that looked like snakes. The Little Mermaid was frightened, but the thought of the prince made her brave.

"I can give you a potion that will make you human," said the Sea Witch. "But if you take it, you will lose your beautiful voice. You will get it back only if you win the true love of the prince."

The Little Mermaid took the potion
from the Sea Witch, and went home to
say goodbye to her father and sisters.

They were sad that she was
leaving, but they all wished her
happiness on land.

"Always remember where you
come from," her father told her,
"and come back to see us once
a year." The Little Mermaid
promised that she would.

Then she drank the witch's
potion and swam to the surface,
where she fell asleep on the soft
sand below the prince's castle.

When the Little Mermaid awoke, her beautiful tail was gone and, in
its place, were two long, slender legs. She was wearing a pretty gown, the
same silvery green as her tail, and on her feet were two silver slippers.

As she tried to stand up, the Little Mermaid's new legs wobbled, and she stumbled.

Suddenly, she was caught by two strong arms. She looked up—right into the eyes of the handsome prince.

"It's you!" the prince cried. "You are the girl who saved me from drowning, aren't you? I have been looking everywhere for you!"

The Little Mermaid nodded. But she could not say a word.

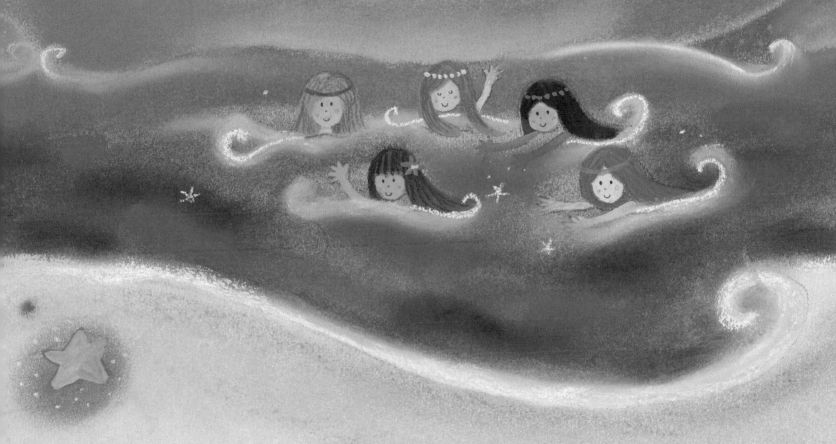

"Why won't you speak to me?" the prince asked, puzzled.

The Little Mermaid couldn't answer. She could only look at the prince and hope that he could see how much she loved him.

And he did. As he gazed into her deep-sea-blue eyes, the prince knew that she was the girl he had been looking for.

"I don't care if you can't speak," he told her. "I know that I love you more than anyone on earth. Will you marry me and live with me forever?"

The Little Mermaid's eyes shone, and she nodded. Then, as the prince kissed her, a wonderful thing happened. She could feel her voice returning!

"Yes," she said happily, "I will marry you!"

They were married the next day, and the Little Mermaid took the name Marina, which means "from the sea."

At their wedding, the prince took her in his arms and whirled her across the sand. Marina's new legs danced beautifully.

Every year on her birthday, Marina went down to the seashore and sang in her beautiful, crystal-clear voice.

Her father and sisters came up to see her, and were glad to know that Marina and her prince would live happily ever after.

The End